A SARALEE SIEGEL BOOK

The Royal Recipe

A Purim Story

W9-CCU-005

By Elana Rubinstein

Illustrated by Jennifer Naalchigar

APPLES & HONEY PRESS

For Pop! Saralee has her Zadie, and I have you.
— E. R.

For Rachel and Macsen.
— J. N.

Apples & Honey Press
An imprint of Behrman House
Millburn, New Jersey 07041
www.applesandhoneypress.com

Text copyright © 2023 by Elana Rubinstein
Illustrations copyright © 2023 by Behrman House

ISBN 978-1-68115-607-1

Library of Congress Cataloging-in-Publication Data
Names: Rubinstein, Elana, author. | Naalchigar, Jennifer, illustrator.
Title: The royal recipe : a Purim story / by Elana Rubinstein ; illustrated
by Jennifer Naalchigar.
Description: Millburn, New Jersey : Apples & Honey Press, [2023] | Series:
Saralee Siegel ; book #4 | Summary: Ten-year-old Saralee Siegal
accidentally summons Haman with her hamantashen recipe, which creates
trouble at Siegel House Restaurant.
Identifiers: LCCN 2022019135 | ISBN 9781681156071 (hardcover)
Subjects: CYAC: Smell--Fiction. | Baking--Fiction. | Grandfathers--Fiction.
| Purim--Fiction. | Restaurants--Fiction. | Jews--United
States--Fiction.
Classification: LCC PZ7.1.R8276 Ro 2023 | DDC [Fic]--dc23
LC record available at https://lccn.loc.gov/2022019135

Design by NeuStudio
Edited by Alef Davis
Printed in China

1 3 5 7 9 8 6 4 2

0223/B2105/A8

Contents

1: Two Peas in a Pod 1

2: Wow Factor 6

3: The Smells of Purim 13

4: Spicy, Tangy, Sweet 19

5: The Party Coordinator 23

6: Always in Character 29

7: Track-Pants Guy 35

8: Purim Spiel 42

9: One True Royal Advisor 48

10: Neigh! 54

11: A Lot in Common 59

12: Hear Ye! Hear Ye! 66

13: The Investigation 73

14: Ting-a-Ling-a-Ling 80

15: Crazy Stories 85

16: Back to His Own Time 93

17: In Your Honor 101

18: Too Much to Handle 106

19: Smell Vortex 113

20: Only You 118

21: The Gift Basket 122

22: The Best Story 127

23: Group Hug 134

24: Together Forever 142

Saralee and Zadie's Hamantashen Recipe 150

Chapter One
Two Peas in a Pod

Here's the truth: my nose is a little bit . . . different.

See, most people can only smell ordinary things—like flowers, and popcorn, and a fresh coat of paint.

But me? I can smell so much *more* than the ordinary.

I have a super-nose. And last week, my nose smelled something out-of-this-world nuts!

It all started when my grandfather and

I were cleaning the kitchen at Siegel House Restaurant. The Jewish holiday of Purim would officially begin in six days, and tomorrow was our big dress rehearsal.

"Now Saralee," said Zadie. "Before everything gets crazy tomorrow, I have a special surprise for you."

I looked up from the dish I was washing. "A surprise?"

Zadie's warm chocolate eyes sparkled. "Yes, but I'm not going to tell you what it is. You'll have to *search* for it, using that super-nose of yours."

I put down the plate and dried my hands. There's nothing I love more than a good smell challenge!

"Okay," I said. "But how do I even know what I'm looking for?"

Zadie chuckled. "Look for something that describes the two of us. That's all I'm going to say."

I closed my eyes and took a deep sniff with

my super-nose. The smells of Siegel House Restaurant swirled into my nostrils.

Something that describes Zadie and me . . .

Baked sweet potato fries? Nope, that definitely wasn't it.

Spicy brown mustard?

Kosher dill pickles?

Fried onions?

Sauerkraut?

Fresh peas . . .

Wait a minute!

My super-nose lingered on the smell of a small peapod somewhere in the house. Zadie always said that the two of us went perfectly together—like two peas in a pod.

Could that be it?

I opened my eyes and followed the scent of the peapod through the Siegel House dining room, which was cluttered with boxes of Purim supplies. Zadie followed me up the stairs to my bedroom.

The scent was stronger up here!

3

I raced to my bed and lifted the pillow. Underneath was an apron in bold reds and blues and purples.

"It matches your Purim costume," said Zadie. "Take a look at the front."

When I turned over the apron, my heart melted like butter in a pan. *Saralee Siegel, Executive Assistant* was embroidered in fancy letters.

"I love it," I squealed. "Thank you, thank you, thank you!"

Even though I'm only ten, I'm Zadie's executive assistant. He's the world's best chef, and I'm the world's best sniffer. Obviously, we make an amazing team.

Underneath the fancy letters was a small pocket. And just as I suspected—a tiny peapod was inside. Zadie gave me a big squeeze. He smelled just as he always did—like peppermint with a hint of corned beef on rye.

"You've been such a big help getting ready for Purim," he said. "Thanks for being my executive assistant. I know I can count on you."

I squeezed him back.

"Of course," I said. "I have the best job in the whole world."

Zadie let go, and I tried on the apron. It fit perfectly. Then I opened the peapod. There were two little peas sitting inside. One was me and the other was Zadie. The two of us would *always* be like that.

Together forever—two peas in a pod.

Chapter Two

Wow Factor

As soon as I woke up the next morning, I could smell Zadie's extra-fluffy chocolate chip pancakes. Yum!

I launched out of bed, threw on my royal costume and brand-new apron, and ran downstairs. It was dress rehearsal day!

Purim is an amazing holiday at Siegel House Restaurant. Everybody wears costumes and tells the story of brave Queen Esther, who saved the Jewish people from the terrible Haman.

But this year, we were trying something new for our celebration. We wanted our guests to feel like they were actually *inside* the Purim story. So we'd decorate the house like an ancient Persian palace and dress up in historical costumes.

The rest of my family was already sitting at the kitchen table. Zadie looked like a king. And my grandmother, whom I call Bubbie, wore her queen outfit: an embroidered nightgown and a tiara decorated with dried noodles.

"Good morning, Pookie Wookie," she said, handing me a plate of pancakes. Bubbie calls everyone Pookie Wookie because she has a hard time remembering names.

"Thanks," I said, taking a sniff.

Of course, my super-nose knew every single ingredient in the pancake recipe: two cups of flour, a cup of milk, an egg, three tablespoons of melted butter, two teaspoons of baking powder, a pinch of salt, a smattering of sugar, and a huge helping of chocolate chips. But before I could get lost in the smells, I felt a poke on my shoulder.

"Check out my awesome new tools," said my little cousin, Josh, showing me his toy doctor's bag. "They're very ancient looking."

I rolled my eyes. Josh is in kindergarten and thinks he's a real doctor. Today he was dressed like a royal physician. His doctor's bag was full of random shapes he'd cut out from cardboard.

"This one's for checking bones." He held up a cardboard strip decorated with skeleton stickers.

"I don't think they had stickers in ancient Persia," I said.

Just then, Zadie cleared his throat. "Good morning, my dearest royal people," he announced in a dramatic voice.

Josh and I giggled. Zadie wanted us to pretend that we were ancient royals during our dress rehearsal. That way we'd have enough practice staying in character for our big event.

"We shall be very busy today," Zadie continued. "We'll be decorating the banquet hall and cooking the royal feast. And alas! Let us not forget about the party coordinator! He shall be here this afternoon to arrange all the banquet details. He'll be lodging with us at Siegel Palace for the rest of the week."

"Good, I'm glad we'll have extra help," said my uncle Sam, drowning his pancakes in syrup. "I bet everyone in town's gonna show up for Purim."

A few droplets of syrup dripped onto the table, and my aunt Bean shot up from her chair.

"Don't move a muscle," she said, grabbing a wet rag to clean the mess.

"Hey, maybe this coordinator will help serve the food too?" yawned my aunt Lotte. "I could seriously use a break."

Everyone chuckled at that. Aunt Lotte was the Siegel House waitress, but she always seemed to be missing whenever the customers wanted to order.

"Hark! You must not forget to use *royal* language today," Zadie reminded us.

"Okay, okay," I laughed. "I mean, why yes, we shall try."

After breakfast, my family began transforming the house into a palace.

Aunt Bean draped silk scarves and twinkly lights from the ceiling. Bubbie glued dried noodles onto a chandelier. Uncle Sam decorated the outside of the house with flags, arches, and banners. Josh set up a royal physician's "office" in the corner of the dining room, with three beanbag chairs for "patients."

And Aunt Lotte . . . she mostly just watched.

Zadie and I worked in the kitchen, of course. We made a few historical dishes: chicken pomegranate stew, cucumber and mint salad, and crispy rice.

But when it came time to make the hamantashen, Zadie frowned.

Hamantashen are the most important part of the Purim menu. They're triangular cookies named for Haman and his three-cornered hat.

"Huh," said Zadie, scratching his head. "Let's take a break from our royal acting to figure out this puzzle. What historical flavors should we put in the hamantashen?"

"Dates and pecans?" I suggested.

Zadie shook his head. "No . . . We need a "wow-factor hamantashen recipe this year. Something with exciting ingredients to bring the Purim story to life!"

"What about sesame paste with chocolate?" I asked.

Zadie shook his head again. "Hmmm, that's not quite it . . . "

My super-nose tingled as an idea formed in my mind. I couldn't believe I hadn't thought of this before!

"Hey, Zadie," I said. "I think I know exactly what we need."

Chapter Three
The Smells of Purim

Zadie's eyes grew wide. "What is it? What should we do?"

By now, I was hopping from foot to foot. This might've been one of my best ideas *ever*.

"Right now, our menu has lots of historically accurate flavors," I said. "But we're *just guessing* what the events in the Purim story smelled like. We don't know for sure."

"Okay . . ." prompted Zadie.

I paused for dramatic effect. Then I said,

"What if I could sniff out the *exact* flavors from the Purim story? What if I could figure out what one of King Ahasuerus's banquets *actually* smelled like?"

Zadie's mouth dropped open.

"But how?" he asked. "How could you possibly smell specific flavors from a story?"

I pointed to my nose. "I have a super-nose, remember? There isn't anything I can't sniff."

Zadie grinned. Then he bonked my nose with his pointer finger. "Now *that's* a wow-factor idea! Alrighty, Saralee, I'll go help with the decorations while you work your magic. Let's see what that super-nose of yours can do!"

Zadie left the kitchen, and I got straight to work on my new hamantashen recipe. I opened the cupboard and looked through the ingredients.

What to pick?

Okay, maybe I had exaggerated a little bit

about my super-smelling abilities. I'd never actually tried smelling something from a story before.

I wiggled my nose a few times, trying to get inspired.

Only nothing happened.

I grabbed a dish towel and tied it around my eyes and ears. See, my nose gets even more powerful when I block out my senses of sight and sound. I call this going into over-smell.

With the world dark and quiet, I could finally concentrate. The first step was to imagine the Purim story. I racked my brain, trying to remember the story details I had learned at school last year.

Ah yes! A Jewish woman named Esther was brought to the king's palace, and she became the new queen.

A few hazy images appeared in my mind. But then they grew clearer and clearer until I felt like I was *actually* there, walking through King Ahasuerus's palace.

Wow!

I was surrounded by ornately decorated walls, tall statues, and elegant serving platters.

Saffron and cardamom

Perfume made from crushed flowers

Pumpkins and pepper

Dried lime

Grape juice

Sweet oils

Hundreds of people swayed and twirled across the dance floor. The king and queen sat on their thrones, surrounded by the royal court.

Beautiful music flowed through the air: melodies made with harps and lutes and drums.

For a moment, I let myself take in all the sights. Then I took a nice, deep sniff.

The smells were unbelievable! They swirled around me, growing stronger by the second. Together, the smells were bold and bright. They changed from sweet, to spicy, to tangy in a fraction of a second. Each flavor was like a note in an ancient song.

I let the smells fill me up. Soon I had all the information I needed for the hamantashen recipe, so the images began to fade. I untied the dish towel and got to work!

My first task was to make a basic hamantashen dough. I mixed the ingredients, rolled the dough flat, and cut out eighteen little circles. Each circle would be its own cookie.

Next it was time for the most important part: the filling. I used chopped walnuts, dates, and pecans as a base. And then I added flavors from the Purim story: a dash of cardamom, a sprinkle of saffron, a pinch of pepper, a squeeze of lime, and a splash of grape juice.

Perfect!

I spooned some filling onto each little circle of dough, folded the edges to make triangles, and slipped the tray into the oven.

Hopefully the extra flavors would bring the smells of the Purim story to life!

Chapter Four
Spicy, Tangy, Sweet

Bing *bing bing*, went the oven timer.

This was it. The moment of truth.

I could already smell a hint of all the special flavors. And when I opened the oven door, an incredible scent washed over me.

The hamantashen smelled bold and bright like the royal banquet hall. The scent was sweet, then spicy, then tangy, before turning sweet again.

I grinned as I set down the tray. My plan had worked!

But . . . what in the world was that?

Hovering above the hamantashen were these weird silver swirls. They curled this way and that, like smoke. But the weirdest part was that tiny images from the Purim story flashed inside: tables covered in food, statues, dancing people, the royal court.

What did these swirls mean?

Before I could get a closer look at the swirls, the kitchen door flew open and my whole family rushed in.

"That smell!" Zadie cried. "Oh Saralee, it's wonderful."

Josh stood on his tippy-toes. "I wanna see!"

"Magnificent," said Aunt Lotte. She licked her lips. "Can't wait to try one."

"Hey, did you guys notice—?" I started.

I looked back at my hamantashen and blinked. The swirls had disappeared.

Huh, that's strange, I thought. *Where did they go?*

"Notice what?" asked Uncle Sam. He walked

over to take a closer look but stubbed his toe on the kitchen island.

"Ouch," he cried, hopping on one foot.

Aunt Bean gave him a look.

Zadie passed out the hamantashen, one for each of us.

"Let's all take a bite on the count of three," he said. "One . . . two . . . three!"

I took a big bite. The cookie was delicious: bold and bright, spicy and sweet. One moment I could taste grapes and cardamom. The next, saffron and lime.

But then, something changed.

I winced as a disgusting flavor hit my tongue. I looked up at my family. They were all puckering their lips.

"Do you taste that?" I asked.

Zadie nodded. "It started off delicious. But there's this terrible aftertaste."

"This tastes even worse than *my* cooking," Aunt Lotte said.

Josh spit out his piece into a paper towel.

21

Then he opened his toy doctor's kit and took out another cardboard tool.

"You didn't pick very good flavors, Saralee," he said. "I think your nose needs an *eezamination.* This tool is called a 'see-up-your-noser.' Okay, tilt your head back."

"Not now, Josh," I huffed.

I couldn't believe this! There was only a hint of that disgusting flavor, but it completely ruined the recipe. My shoulders slumped.

Zadie wrapped his arm around me.

"Now don't you worry," he said. "There's still plenty of time to tweak the recipe before Purim. Mistakes are a part of the process. For now, it's wonderful that you were able to bring the smells of the Purim story to—"

Knock, knock.

We all glanced at each other.

There was someone at the door.

Chapter Five
The Party Coordinator

Zadie opened the front door, and I blinked a few times. This was definitely NOT what I was expecting.

The man on the front step was also dressed in a historical costume, but his outfit was much fancier than ours. A red robe with golden embroidery fell to his ankles. Brightly colored rings gleamed on his fingers. He seemed familiar, though I wasn't sure how.

"Wow," said Zadie. "Look at that outfit. You must be the party coordinator!"

The man frowned at us.

"Your castle is on such a strange-looking road," he said gruffly. "What kingdom is this?"

Zadie grinned and turned to the rest of us.

"This guy is a professional," he whispered. "He's *already* acting like an ancient guy. Amazing!"

Zadie turned back to the party coordinator.

"This is Siegel Palace, of course," he boomed, ushering the man into the house. "The best palace in all of Persia. As king, I welcome you to our home."

The party coordinator actually *bowed* to Zadie. "My king, I am honored to be your chief royal adviser."

Zadie chuckled again. Then he turned back to us and whispered, "By golly, he's good. Get it? There weren't any party coordinators back in the Purim days. Chief royal advisor is so much more historically accurate."

Everyone else laughed. But I didn't think it was *that* funny.

"Now, let me introduce you to my fam—I mean, my *royal court*." Zadie gestured to all of us. "There's Bean, Sam, Lotte, Josh and Saralee." He paused to put his arm around Bubbie. "And this is my lovely queen, Ruth Anne."

"Pleasure to meet you, Pookie Wookie," Bubbie said.

"I love your outfit!" gushed Aunt Bean. "Look at those stitches. So tiny and perfect. And you don't have a single stain!"

She looked pointedly at Uncle Sam, whose robe already had three stains on it.

"I'm the royal physician," Josh piped up. "I will cure you of the measles and the small pockets."

The party coordinator scratched his chin. "You mean smallpox. Yes, that's a terrible disease in my kingdom."

Even Aunt Lotte was excited to meet the new guy. "It's great that you're here. I have a whole list of things you can help me with, Mr. . . ."

Zadie smacked his forehead. "My goodness, how rude of us! Pray tell, what is your name kind sir?"

The man bowed again. "Your Highness, my name is H—"

CRASH!

We all whirled around to see Uncle Sam hopping on one foot again. He'd bumped into a decorative urn, and the whole thing had cracked into pieces.

"Oh snickerdoodle," Uncle Sam mumbled. "It's the same toe I stubbed before."

Aunt Bean sighed. "What a mess! I'll get the broom." She dashed into the kitchen.

"I'm sorry about that," chuckled Zadie, as Aunt Bean swept up the shards. "You'll find that it's never boring at Siegel Palace. But your name is Herman, you say? Well, it's nice to meet you, Herman! Now who hasn't had a chance to say hello yet. Oh, Saralee—"

Zadie put his hands on my shoulders. "Now Herman, Saralee is very important. She's my executive assistant."

Herman peered down at me. "My king, what is an . . . *executive assistant?*"

"Saralee helps me keep this place running smoothly," Zadie explained.

Herman still looked confused, so I decided to just put it in ancient terms.

"It's basically the same thing as a chief royal advisor," I said. "Zadie and I make decisions together."

Herman frowned at Zadie. "So you have *two* chief royal advisors in this palace? How very . . . untraditional. And I've never seen such a small chief royal advisor before."

Small? Excuse me?

But Zadie just laughed and slapped his knee. "You're a riot, Herman. I'm telling you, Saralee may be young, but she sure is mighty. You'll see. Well, now that you know everyone, I think it's time for an official tour."

I crossed my arms. This party coordinator seemed kinda *rude*. I tried to catch Zadie's eye, but he was already leading Herman into the dining room.

Chapter Six
Always in Character

"As you can see, this is our ancient banquet hall," Zadie said.

Herman stroked his beard as he gazed around the room. "But where is your throne, my king? All kings and queens *must* have royal thrones. Here—"

He strode to the center of the room and pulled two chairs from the table. Then he found a box full of silk scarves.

We watched in amazement as Herman

expertly wrapped the chairs in the scarves. When he was done, the chairs looked like thrones, fit for a real king and queen.

"Your majesties, please be seated," Herman said to Bubbie and Zadie. "Kings and queens must recline in the most elaborate chairs. It is the custom."

Herman guided Bubbie and Zadie to their new thrones.

"My stars, Pookie Wookie," Bubbie gushed. "How wonderful."

Zadie leaned back in his new seat. "Goodness, Herman, thank you so much. We completely forgot about having thrones. Now I'm wondering what other details we've forgotten."

"With me, nothing is forgotten," said Herman, tilting up his chin. "I will address every detail, no matter how small! There is no need to fret, my king."

My throat felt dry all of a sudden. Herman's thrones had turned out so nice. Meanwhile, my Royal Hamantashen were just so . . . gross!

Even though Zadie said it was okay to make mistakes, I didn't feel good watching Herman show off his historical knowledge.

Zadie closed his eyes and settled deeper into his throne. Aunt Bean tapped him on the shoulder.

"We're in the middle of the tour," she whispered. "Remember?"

Zadie popped up from his chair. "Oh yes, yes. Come on, guys, let's show Herman where the real magic happens."

When Zadie led us into the kitchen, Herman's mouth fell open.

"What is this room?" he gasped. "And what is that silver contraption?"

Everyone burst into laughter.

"That, my dear chief royal advisor, is called a refrigerator," said Zadie. "It keeps our food cold so it lasts longer."

Herman's eyes widened. "My king, though your palace is small, you have riches beyond measure."

Zadie stared at the refrigerator.

"Hold on a minute, where's the ice cream maker?" he asked. "It was right on top of the fridge this morning. Bean, did you reorganize in here?"

"Not today," said Aunt Bean. "And I keep the ice cream maker on top of the fridge. It's the only place where it fits."

Zadie scratched his chin. "Never mind. I'm sure it just got moved around. Let's continue the kitchen tour."

I leaned over to whisper to Zadie. "But what about my Royal Hamantashen? I need to use the kitchen to fix the recipe."

"Don't worry," he whispered back. "You can work on your recipe later. It's not every day we get to interact with such a historical expert. "

He turned back to Herman. "Now, if you love the refrigerator, just wait until you hear about the freezer!"

The tour went on and on. Herman pretended to be confused about *everything* in the kitchen! Apparently ancient people have never heard of blenders, tea kettles, paper napkins, or toasters.

After a while, everyone sat at the kitchen island to ask Herman questions about ancient details for the Purim party.

"What type of jewelry should we wear?" asked Aunt Bean.

"Maybe you'll set the tables instead of me," said Aunt Lotte. "I bet you know how to do it correctly."

"Golly," said Zadie. "You're so knowledgeable, Herman. You must have done so much research to prepare for this job."

"Yes, my king," Herman said. "I keep up to date with the most important scrolls so I can advise your majesty appropriately."

Zadie shook his head in amazement. "Now that you're here, our party will *definitely* be historically accurate! I want to get every detail right. What can you tell me about ancient cooking practices?"

Hold on, what?

Herman was only here to coordinate the party details. He wasn't supposed to help in the kitchen! That was *my* special job with Zadie.

"Wait, Zadie—" I started.

But Herman was talking so loudly that Zadie didn't hear me.

Ugh, I couldn't stand this anymore! I stomped upstairs to my room. I thought that Zadie would notice I was gone, but he never did.

Chapter Seven
Track-Pants Guy

The next morning, I took a nice, deep sniff as soon as I woke up.

Hmmm ... Something was off.

I didn't smell any of Zadie's usual breakfast items: eggs with toast, or pancakes, or waffles. Today, the smells were totally different—like some sort of bread.

After getting dressed, I dashed downstairs to investigate. "Morning," I said, opening the door to the kitchen. "What's—"

I froze. Zadie was standing at the stove with Herman. The guy was STILL wearing his ancient costume, even though the dress rehearsal was over. Unbelievable!

"Good morning, Saralee," said Zadie. "Herman's showing me how to make ancient flatbreads."

Zadie took a flatbread off the pile and put it on a plate for me.

"Look, there's lots of things to dip it into," he said. "We've got cheese, honey, and jam."

"But . . . but why are you cooking with Herman?" I whispered to him. "That's something *we* do together."

"It's all right, Saralee," Zadie whispered back. "Herman's on a roll. I've never met such a dedicated actor. He wanted to 'try out' a modern kitchen appliance. Plus, we can work together on your Royal Hamantashen this afternoon."

"I just don't understand, my king," called Herman, flipping another flatbread. "Where's the fire that gives this oven warmth?"

Zadie chuckled. "Herman, you're a riot."

36

Soon the rest of my family came downstairs for breakfast.

"Smells good in here," said Uncle Sam.

"Sure does," mumbled Aunt Lotte, rubbing her eyes. "Where's the coffee?"

"You have the strangest fashion in this kingdom," Herman said, frowning at her bedazzled jeans.

"You're just hilarious, Herman," Aunt Bean laughed. She took a flatbread for herself.

"This is exceptional," Uncle Sam said through a mouthful of flatbread. He put three more pieces on his plate.

Why was everyone so excited about Herman's flatbreads? I mean, they didn't smell *that* good! He'd used a super basic recipe: two cups of flour, two tablespoons of butter, two-thirds cup of milk, and a half teaspoon of salt. There wasn't anything special about that!

Josh shoved his ancient physician costume onto my lap. "Saralee, it won't fit in my backpack," he said. "Can you help?"

"Why do you need it?" I asked.

"We're doing a Purim skit at school today," he explained. "I'm supposed to be a royal guard, but I want to be a royal physician and bring this costume instead."

I jammed his robe into his backpack. There wasn't actually a royal physician in the Purim story. But Josh *always* has to be a doctor, no matter what.

"Okay, let's go," I said. I didn't want to spend any more time with Herman.

"Aren't you having breakfast?" Zadie asked.

"I'm not hungry," I mumbled.

As Josh and I walked to the door, something rumbled outside—as if a car was pulling up our driveway.

Huh, that's strange, I thought. We weren't expecting anyone.

When I opened the door, a man was on the front steps. He wore track pants and a T-shirt that said *PPP*. He carried a big duffel bag over his shoulder.

"Is this Siegel House Restaurant?" he asked.

Josh waved around a cardboard tool. "No, this is Siegel *Palace*. I'm the royal physician. Before you come in, I have to test you for the measles."

The man frowned at Josh. "I don't get it. Is this Siegel House or not?"

I nodded. "Sorry, he's just playing around."

The man let out a big sigh. "I'm so sorry I'm late. I'm from Playful Party Planners. I was supposed to be here yesterday, but I got a flat tire and then my engine died. It was awful."

Wait . . . there was *another* party coordinator?

"I tried calling a bunch of times," the man continued. "But no one picked up the phone."

"Oh," I said. "Yesterday we had our dress rehearsal, so we turned off our phones to be more historically accurate. But Herman's here already."

"Herman?" asked the man. "Who's—"

"Hi there." Zadie had come to the door. "Can I help you?"

Again, the man explained about his car troubles.

"Oh golly, I'm so sorry," Zadie said. "I think the company must have asked both of you by mistake. Herman's really prepared for the job. I'm so sorry you came all this way."

The man blinked a few times.

"Sheesh, in all my years, this has never happened before," he muttered. "I guess . . . I guess I'll go. Have a nice holiday."

The man shuffled back to his car.

This whole thing seemed off to me. How could the party planning service have sent two people by accident? Something fishy was going on.

"Zadie," I started. "About Herman. Do you think that there's something, I don't know . . . odd about him?"

Zadie wrinkled his eyebrows. "Odd? What do you mean?"

"Well, why is he *still* acting like an ancient guy?" I asked. "Our dress rehearsal is over. And why isn't he wearing the Playful Party Planners uniform? That other coordinator had one."

Zadie patted my shoulder. "I think Herman is just really dedicated to the royalty theme. I know it's hard to have someone new around, but let's try to make him feel welcome. He'll probably relax and show us his real personality when he's more comfortable."

I let out a big sigh. Herman was over-the-top, but maybe Zadie was right. Maybe I was just jealous because Zadie liked him so much. And if Zadie trusted him, I should trust him too.

Purim Spiel

At school, I plopped down next to my best friend, Harold Horowitz. Today he wore a button-down shirt with a polka-dot tie.

"Oh my goodness, Saralee," he said, "you'll never believe the theme my family chose for our big Purim lunch."

Harold's family owns the other restaurant in town, Perfection on a Platter. This year, Siegel House would host the official Purim dinner, while Harold's restaurant would host a big lunch the next day. That way everyone in town could go to *both* restaurants for the holiday.

"What is it?" I asked.

Harold grinned, revealing his shiny blue braces. "It's a fairy-tale theme. But all my relatives want to dress up like villains. No princesses or fairy godmothers at Perfection on a Platter, that's for sure! I'm going to be the giant from Jack and the Beanstalk."

I laughed. Harold's family could be a little . . . *intense.*

"So what's going on at Siegel House?" Harold asked. "Are you guys still doing a historical royal experience?"

"Yeah, Zadie hired this party coordinator to help with our event," I said. "And he's obsessed with staying in character as an ancient guy. He won't drop the act for a second."

"Sounds dramatic," said Harold.

"Tell me about it," I said. "But things haven't been going so well."

I explained how I made a new hamantashen

recipe to bring the smells of the Purim story to life.

"It's the craziest thing," I said. "At first, they tasted delicious. But then this terrible aftertaste took over. I don't know how to fix them!"

Briiiiiiiiiing! went the morning bell.

"I bet you'll figure it out in time for Purim," Harold whispered.

"Let's hope so," I whispered back.

Our teacher, Mrs. Stearns, walked to the front of the room.

"Good morning, everyone," she said. "Today we have a special presentation from the

kindergarten class. They're going to perform the Purim story for us."

The kindergarten teacher led her class into the room.

"Hey, Saralee!" Josh called, holding up his toy doctor's bag.

"Long, long ago, in Shushan," said the teacher, "there lived a king who liked to throw lots of parties."

"And also in Shushan, there was a very brave royal physician," said Josh, waving his see-up-your-noser.

Everyone in my class giggled. The

kindergarten teacher's face turned bright red, and she gave Josh a look.

"Now, the king had an advisor named Haman," the teacher continued. "Haman was a proud, self-absorbed man."

The little kindergartner Haman was scowling but still looked super-cute.

"Bow to me, Mordecai," Haman said. "I am the king's chief royal advisor!"

"Never," said the kindergartener Mordecai. "I am Jewish. And I only bow to God."

"I will get revenge on you and all of your people," cried the cute little Haman. "I will tell the king to get rid of you all."

My class cheered when brave Queen Esther saved all the Jews and got rid of Haman instead. The kindergarteners waved goodbye, and Josh held up his see-up-your-noser like a sword.

"Royal doctor to the rescue," he called.

His teacher ushered the kindergarteners out the door, but Josh kept poking his head back in and waving to me and Harold.

"All right everyone, open your vocabulary books to page 131," said Mrs. Stearns.

But as we went over the answers to the homework, I couldn't concentrate.

During the Purim play, Haman kept calling himself the chief royal advisor. And that was exactly what Herman called *himself*.

Maybe Herman was using Haman as inspiration for his acting. That would explain his behavior—right?

Chapter Nine
One True Royal Advisor

On the way home from school, Josh kept stopping to wave around the tools from his doctor's bag.

"Can you please hurry up?" I asked. "I need to work on my hamantashen recipe with Zadie."

"Wasn't I a great royal doctor this morning?" he asked, holding up the see-up-your-noser.

"Yes, yes, you were great," I muttered. "Come on, we're almost there."

But when we got home, there was the strangest sight on the front lawn.

Herman was surrounded by bowling pins and beanbags. He was pacing back and forth, muttering to himself. He kicked a beanbag, then tried to balance two bowling pins on top of each other.

"What's he doing?" whispered Josh.

"I don't know," I whispered back.

Herman looked up at us. His face was red, and his beard was sticking out in all directions.

"Oh, tiny servants," he said. "Fetch me new statues this instant." He gestured to the bowling pins. "These are completely useless."

Josh and I glanced at each other. Yesterday he'd been just a little bit rude to me. But this was way worse!

"Excuse me, are you talking to *us*?" I asked. "We're not servants. Remember, I'm Zadie's executive assistant. And those are bowling pins, not statues."

Herman's face got even redder.

"What disrespect!" he growled. "The king only has ONE true chief royal advisor. And that's *me*."

I felt like someone had dropped a sack of potatoes onto my stomach. Herman was like a completely different person today. He wasn't just rude; he was *super-mean!*

"You can't talk to us like that!" I said.

"Yeah, I'm a royal doctor," Josh said. "I'm important!"

Herman rolled back his shoulders and puffed out his chest.

"Such incompetence," he muttered. "Now I'll have to get the statues myself." He turned and strutted inside.

My blood boiled as Josh and I followed Herman into the house. Why was Herman acting like this? I needed to tell Zadie immediately.

But as soon as he entered the dining room, Herman turned back into the "nice" guy from yesterday.

"Oh, my king," he called. His words were sticky and sweet, like super-sugary icing. "I humbly request your royal presence."

Zadie was lounging on his new throne. "What's up, Herman? Oh hey, kids!"

"Zadie, I need to talk to you," I said.

"Yeah," said Josh. "We need to tell you about Herm—"

But Herman stepped in front of us, blocking us from Zadie's view. "My dearest king, the statues outside must be replaced. You deserve so much better."

Zadie furrowed his eyebrows. "Statues?"

I knew exactly what was going on! Around grownups, Herman acted so nice and helpful. But when they weren't around, his real personality came out. And Zadie had no idea!

"Zadie, can we talk for a—"

"Your Highness," interrupted Herman, "if you are so inclined, please accompany me to the outskirts of the palace."

"Hold on a minute, Herman," said Zadie. "I think Saralee is trying to say something."

Finally! "Yeah, just now, when Josh and I were outside—"

Herman gasped and pointed to the fancy candles on the table.

"My king, look over there!" he cried. "These adornments aren't right. They need more height, more drama."

This was getting ridiculous. Herman wouldn't let me say a word to Zadie! My hands balled into fists. I needed to get Zadie alone so I could tell him about Herman's mean side.

By this point, Josh had lost interest and went to play in his ancient physician's office.

"Zadie, it's time to work on the hamantashen," I said.

"Hold on, Saralee." Zadie turned back to Herman. "You have a point, Herman. Is there a way we can make the candles more accurate for the time period?"

"My king, you are the greatest ruler this land has ever seen," Herman said smoothly. "You must have the most spectacular adornments. Please, follow me. I saw a chest of embellishments over here—"

Herman beckoned Zadie toward a box in the corner.

"Hey, what about the hamantashen?" I asked.

Zadie turned around. "Oh yes, Saralee. Give me a little while to fix these decorations and then we'll bake together, okay? And I should see about those . . . *statues* too. I just want to make sure everything is perfect for our party."

"Wait, can't we—" I started.

"So what do you think, Herman?" asked Zadie, digging through the box of decorations. "Should we put out lanterns instead of candles?"

There was no use trying to get Zadie's attention. So I walked to the kitchen *alone*.

Chapter Ten
Neigh!

My executive-assistant apron hung on a peg in the kitchen. For the first time, it felt itchy against my skin.

This whole "mean Herman" situation really bothered me. Zadie was so focused on making our Purim party historically accurate that he couldn't see Herman's true personality. It felt like *Herman* was Zadie's executive assistant now.

I swallowed hard. I needed to fix my Royal Hamantashen recipe so I could bring the smells and tastes of Purim to Siegel Palace *myself.* Hopefully this would show Zadie that we didn't need Herman's help. We could have an amazing party without him!

I tied a dish towel around my eyes and ears and went into over-smell. I imagined the Purim story, and scenes came into focus.

This time, I saw the royal courtyard. Parrots swooped above patches of sweet-smelling roses. A man rode a black horse through a garden path. Some women in long dresses strolled across the terrace, and some sat for cake and tea. A soft breeze carried the scents of rose petals, ginger, cinnamon tea, and almond cake drizzled with syrup.

Aha!

I ripped off the dish towel and gathered my ingredients. My hamantashen filling would be the same as yesterday, only this time I'd add a pinch of cinnamon, a drizzle of almond extract, a splash of rose water, and a hint of ginger. These sweet flavors would get rid of that disgusting aftertaste for sure!

Thirty minutes later, the hamantashen were baked to a golden brown. When I opened the oven door, an incredible smell flooded the kitchen.

But then . . .

I saw them again—those *swirls*. They were even larger than last time! Hazy images floated inside: bright flowers, squawking parrots, women in dresses, and a black horse.

I squinted at the swirls. But before I could make sense of the images, the swirls disappeared.

I didn't understand it. What could these swirls mean? Something strange was going on with this recipe. But what could I do now that the swirls were gone?

I plucked a cookie off the tray and took a bite. It tasted heavenly. Once again the taste kept changing, this time from almond, to lime, to cinnamon, to saffron, to . . .

"Ugh!" I spat out the mouthful.

That terrible aftertaste was back. And this time it was even stronger! Why did this keep happening? How had that rotten flavor gotten in there? This whole thing was so frustrat—

Neeeeeeiiiiiigggggggghhhhhh!

I froze. "What in the world?"

Neeeeeeiiiiiigggggggghhhhhh!

I rushed to the front door. The rest of my family must have heard the noise as well, because they followed right behind.

"What's going on?" asked Aunt Bean.

Uncle Sam almost tripped over a chair to get to the door. "Yeah, what's—"

Neeeeeeiiiiiigggggghhhhhh!

I opened the door and—

"Oh my goodness," I breathed.

Standing on our front lawn was a beautiful black horse.

Chapter Eleven
A Lot in Common

The horse's reins sparkled with jewels, and his saddle was made from fine leather. The horse tossed his head gracefully, then nibbled the grass.

My relatives swarmed around the horse, but I couldn't move. I was frozen to the spot!

Zadie clapped Herman on the back. "Herman, this is incredible. You arranged a royal horse? Now the kids can have horseback rides!"

59

Herman bowed. "My king, the royal horse of Shushan is the fastest horse in all the land."

Aunt Lotte stroked the horse's mane. She looked *way* less cranky than normal. "Hi there, sweet horsey," she cooed.

Josh examined the horse's ears with one of his cardboard tools. "Wave your tail if you can hear me," he said softly. "This is a hearing test. Hellooooooooo!"

The horse perked up his ears and swished his tail.

"Wow, do you think he can understand me?" Josh cried. "This horse is so smart!"

Zadie called over to me. "Saralee, come and meet the royal horse!"

In a daze, I approached the horse and touched his muzzle. He nestled his nose into the crook of my arm.

This was just too weird! I'd seen a horse just like this in the smell swirls, and now there was a real live horse here at Siegel House. Could that really be a coincidence?

Wait a minute!

A CRAZY thought flew into my mind. Could this be the same horse I'd seen in the swirls? Had my super-nose accidentally brought it here?

It seemed impossible, but my super-nose has done some pretty unbelievable things. Last fall, I smelled a flavor from outer space. And last winter, my super-nose took me time traveling. Maybe my nose was doing the opposite now: bringing things from the past into the present.

But this wasn't the first time I'd made the Royal Hamantashen recipe. Had I summoned something from the Purim story yesterday, too, when I saw the king's royal banquet?

Well, nothing strange showed up yester—

"My king, would you like to sit on the royal horse?" Herman asked Zadie.

"Absolutely," Zadie replied.

I stared at Herman.

No . . . it couldn't be!

Herman seemed *really* committed to acting like an ancient person. But this morning, a man from Playful Party Planners showed up claiming to be the real party coordinator. Maybe Herman wasn't who we thought he was. Maybe he was from the Purim story, just like the horse!

Herman helped Zadie climb into the saddle.

"Your Majesty, it is an honor to see you on the royal steed," boomed Herman. "You look so dignified! So regal! It is my pleasure to serve as your *chief royal advisor.*" He shot me a look.

"Why thank you, Herman," said Zadie.

Goosebumps rose on my arms.

Why was Herman being so competitive with me? It was like he wanted to steal my job as executive assistant and keep all the power to himself.

My stomach dropped.

There was someone in the Purim story who acted just like that—Haman!

I thought back to yesterday when I'd seen the swirls for the first time. I'd seen the king surrounded by five men of his royal court. Could one of those men have been Haman?

There were a lot of similarities, after all.

Herman kept calling himself "chief royal advisor," just like Haman.

Like Haman, Herman was nasty to people

he thought were beneath him. And he wanted to take my place as Zadie's second in command.

Even their names sounded similar!

My stomach churned as I watched Zadie and Herman. My grandfather looked so happy as he paraded up and down the driveway on the royal horse.

"Wheeeeee!" he cheered.

"Hey," said Aunt Bean. "Where did my big flowerpot go? It was right here on the front step. It had all my daffodils in it!"

But nobody paid much attention to the missing flowerpot. Everyone was still super-excited about the horse.

Herman helped Zadie dismount, and I let out a breath.

Okay, maybe I was getting a little carried away.

Sure, Herman might've been rude to me earlier. But that didn't make him Haman! And sure, this horse looked super-fancy. But that didn't mean this was the *same exact* fancy horse from the Purim story. Plus, Haman always wore a triangular hat, and Herman didn't have one of those.

I was probably letting my imagination get carried away. But still . . . I had a terrible feeling that I just couldn't shake.

Chapter Twelve
Hear Ye! Hear Ye!

The next morning, Zadie and Herman baked flatbreads together *again*.

"Kids, I had the best idea," said Zadie. "Today Herman will take you to school—*on the royal horse.* It will be like an advertisement for our big party."

Josh glanced nervously at Herman. But I could tell he was still excited about the horse ride.

"Did you know that *waaaaay* back in time,

doctors rode horses to visit sick people?" he asked me. "It's because there weren't any cars."

"Yeah, great," I said.

I glared at Herman. He glared back.

Herman was probably upset that he'd have to spend so much time with two "tiny servants." Well, I wasn't so excited about it either.

"But Zadie," I started. "We can't—"

"Don't worry, it's totally safe," Zadie said. "Herman knows everything there is to know about horses."

So after breakfast, Herman helped Josh and me onto the royal horse. Since Zadie was watching, he did it with a fake smile on his face.

"Up you go," Herman said through gritted teeth. His hands were freezing, *like ice.*

I scowled as he took the reins. I didn't trust him to keep us safe once the grownups weren't around. I held tight to the front of the saddle as the horse began to trot.

Clickety-clack.

Clickety-clack.

"Such a waste of time," Herman muttered. "I have important advisor duties today."

At the sound of Herman's voice, the horse pinned back his ears and let out a big snuff. Good—the horse didn't like Herman either!

"Hear ye! Hear ye!" Josh called. "Come to Siegel House for Purim. Hear ye! Hear ye!"

"I'll be there!" called Mr. Alkana from his front lawn.

Mrs. Baum clapped her hands from her porch. "Amazing horse! You guys really went all out."

Herman's face grew red.

Hear ye!
Hear ye!

"This is humiliating," he hissed. "This horse is meant for kings and queens. Not the likes of you."

"You better stop calling us servants," I hissed back. "Kids aren't servants, especially at Siegel Palace."

"Yeah!" chimed in Josh. "I'm not a servant. I'm a royal doctor."

Herman's face got even redder. "How dare you talk to me in that manner. I'm the king's chief royal advisor. The king may *think* you're important. But I know the truth—the two of you are just teeny tiny servants with no power at all. He'll see the truth soon, just you wait."

"You will never EVER be Zadie's chief royal advisor!" I cried. "That's my job now and forever."

Herman's lips curled. "I've put up with this disrespect long enough. Mark my words, little servant, I'll have my revenge."

I shivered.

If this guy truly was Haman, he wasn't

kidding. In the Purim story, Haman tried to get revenge on the Jews after Mordecai refused to bow to him. He told the king to get rid of the Jewish people forever—and the king actually listened. It wasn't until Queen Esther revealed that she was Jewish that the king realized his mistake.

By now we were close to the school's entrance. The horse whinnied, and a crowd of kids gathered around us.

"What a cute horse," gushed Rachel Rubin.

"Get out of my way," Herman shouted. The kids scattered as Herman brought the horse to a stop. Everyone laughed nervously as Josh and I dismounted.

"What an actor!" Jacob Brodsky shouted. "I've heard about the Siegel House Purim event. But this is even cooler than I thought."

Rachel reached out to pet the horse, but Herman swatted her hand away.

"Stay away, you tiny servant," he hissed.

Rachel's cheeks turned bright red.

Jacob Brodsky laughed. "He's just acting, right, Saralee?"

"Ummm . . ."

The horse nuzzled the top of Rachel's head while Herman glowered at the kids. "All you tiny servants, don't you have work to do? How dare you gaze in my direction. Get back to your duties!"

Then he swung himself onto the saddle and rode away.

The horse cast a longing look back at me. Poor guy!

Harold came over as everyone else headed to class. "Wow, that guy is terrifying. He's definitely using Haman as inspiration for his acting, that's for sure."

"It might be worse than that," I said in a low voice. "Remember how I told you about that hamantashen recipe with the smells of the Purim story? Well, I'm worried that my super-nose has been accidentally summoning *things* out of the Purim story too."

71

"What do you mean?" asked Harold.

"Yesterday that horse showed up right after I'd made those hamantashen," I explained. "What if it's the real royal horse from the Purim story? And the day before, when I made the hamantashen for the first time, Herman showed up. I think he's actually HAMAN!"

Harold raised an eyebrow. "For real?"

I nodded.

"But Saralee . . . that seems kind of impossible," Harold said slowly. "Don't you think he's just getting into character? You should see my family—they've been acting like fairy-tale villains all week."

"Harold, I'm serious. I don't think he's just acting."

Harold adjusted his glasses. "Let's investigate this. You can make your hamantashen recipe again, and if something else gets summoned from the story, we'll know Herman is actually Haman. But if nothing happens, then we'll know all of this was just in your imagination."

Chapter Thirteen
The Investigation

When Harold, Josh, and I got home, Herman and Zadie were on the front lawn with the royal horse. Herman was trying to brush out the horse's mane, but the horse kept darting away from him.

"Perhaps you should hire a groomer to take care of the horse, my king," said Herman.

"Great idea," Zadie said. "Let's put Lotte in charge of that. The horse seems to love her."

"Hi, Zadie," I called.

Zadie looked up. "Oh hey, kiddos. How was your—"

"Oh my king, how will the esteemed guests enter the banquet?" interrupted Herman. "Shall a squire announce their names?"

Zadie turned back to Herman. "Now that's an idea! Maybe we could . . . "

Ugh. Zadie *still* didn't seem to notice that Herman was taking up all of his time.

"Zadie, look what I made today," said Josh. He walked toward Zadie on the lawn, holding one of his art projects. But Herman glared at him when Zadie's back was turned.

Josh backed up a few steps and frowned. "You know what, it's time for my stuffies to take their medicine," he said. "See you later."

"This is what I'm talking about," I muttered to Harold. "Herman won't let us talk to Zadie at all."

We headed inside to start our investigation

"So Herman and Zadie are close friends now?" Harold asked as we mixed the hamantashen dough.

I added a little more flour to the bowl. "Yeah, that's the problem. Zadie wants every detail of this party to be perfect. He's been asking Herman questions about historical stuff non-stop. And Herman loves all the attention!"

"Doesn't he know how nasty Herman really is?" Harold asked.

I shook my head. "He has no idea. I want to tell him, but Herman keeps getting in the way."

With the dough complete, it was time to go into over-smell and make my hamantashen filling.

"I'm going to imagine the Purim story," I explained. "That will give me a bunch of flavor ideas. I'll list out the ingredients. Will you grab them from the cupboard?"

"Sure," said Harold.

Once again, I tied the dish towel around my eyes and ears, and images from the Purim story came into focus.

This time, I found myself in the royal performance hall. Party guests lounged on woven rugs. Servants bustled around with trays of mouthwatering food. A group of jesters did somersaults onstage and burst into song. The crowd cheered.

My super-nose tingled and I took a deep sniff.

"Orange zest," I called to Harold. "Cherries, fresh mint, nutmeg, cloves, and pomegranate."

"Whoa, slow down," Harold called back. His voice sounded far away, as if he was shouting through a tunnel.

But I didn't have time to repeat myself. New scents swirled into my nostrils.

"Oooh, lemon juice, raisins, and pistachios," I added.

My nose was full of flavors now, and the images began to fade. I took off the dish towel to find Harold scurrying around the kitchen, his arms full of fruits and spices.

"What did you see?" he asked.

"A big party," I said. "With servants and jesters and a huge crowd of guests."

"I wish I could've seen that," Harold sighed. "You have the coolest nose ever, Saralee."

When we found all the ingredients, Harold helped me make the filling. Then we filled each cookie and folded it into a triangle.

"So what happens now?" he asked.

I stuck the tray into the oven. "We wait. And when the hamantashen are done, we'll know the truth."

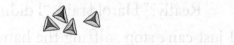

Beeeeeeeep!

"I should warn you," I said, slipping on my pot holders. "This recipe smells . . . *intense.*"

"I'm ready for it," said Harold.

I opened the oven door, and an incredible scent filled every nook and cranny of the kitchen.

"Wow," breathed Harold. "It's really like we're in the Purim story. I can see the story in my head whenever I take a sniff."

He grabbed two cups from the cabinet and filled them with water. And that's when those silver swirls appeared again. This time I could see the faint outline of servants with trays of food, laughing guests, and dancing jesters.

"Look, Harold," I cried, pointing to the swirls.

Harold turned around. "What?"

But the swirls had already disappeared.

"They were just there!" I huffed. "Swirls with images inside. They always show up when I make this recipe."

"Really?" Harold said. "I didn't see anything. I just can't stop sniffing the hamantashen. Can we try one now? I'm dying to have a taste."

"I guess we should," I said.

We each picked up a cookie. I took just a teeny tiny little nibble, but my tongue exploded with flavors: sweet, spicy, tangy.

"Oh wow, it tastes so—" Harold froze and his face turned a light shade of green. He spit his piece into his hand.

I cringed as that horrible flavor hit my tongue. I spit out my piece as well and grabbed a cup of water.

"Gosh, that's terrible," said Harold. "I don't think you should serve these at the—"

CRASH!

Harold's eyes grew wide. "What was that?"

"No idea," I said. "It came from the dining room—come on!"

Chapter Fourteen
Ting-a-Ling-a-Ling

No, no, no, NO!!!

In the Siegel House dining room were three *jesters*! One jester danced on top of the table. Another juggled spoons. And a third played an ancient-looking instrument.

Harold stared at me. "Y-you said you saw jesters when you imagined the P-purim story," he spluttered. "Could this . . . Saralee, these jesters are from . . . "

"I know," I said.

I didn't want to believe it, but this was the evidence I needed. First Herman had appeared out of nowhere, then the royal horse, and now three jesters. My super-nose really was summoning things from the Purim story.

My family and Herman burst into the dining room. Everyone's mouths fell open.

"What's going on?" asked Aunt Bean.

"My goodness, Herman," said Zadie. "You brought royal jesters as well? Now we have a royal horse *and* great entertainment for the party. I am just thrilled!"

Herman scratched his chin, his eyebrows squished together. Then his face relaxed into a charming smile. "Of course, my king. Jesters are an important part of every great royal banquet."

My hands grew cold and clammy. Herman wasn't a party coordinator. And he wasn't pretending to be an ancient guy either. He actually WAS an ancient guy. He was the terrible Haman!

The jesters started singing at the top of their lungs:

Bells, bells, our hats have bells
Ting-a-ling-a-ling, oh so merry
We'll do a little jig, and a flip, and a song
Come and celebrate, and don't you tarry.

Aunt Lotte put her hands over her ears. "Please tell me I don't have to listen to this until Purim."

Josh tried poking one of the jesters with a cardboard tool, but the jester leapt away before Josh could do an official doctor examination.

"Stay still," Josh cried, chasing after him. "This will only be a pinch."

Meanwhile, Bubbie clapped her hands to the song. "Keep going, Pookie Wookies. What a treat!"

"You know, Herman," Zadie shouted over the noise, "you're just incredible. When this holiday is over, I want you to come work for us full-time."

I froze. Had I heard correctly? Zadie wanted Haman to work for Siegel House *FULL-TIME?*

Haman bowed to Zadie. "Of course, my king. It would be my honor to work as your chief royal advisor—*permanently.*" He shot me a triumphant look.

Suddenly, I didn't care that Haman was a super-villain and I was just a ten-year-old kid. I'd had enough of him trying to come between me and Zadie. He thought he could take my place? Well, I'd show him!

The jesters pranced around us.

Fa-la-la-la-la, an advisor for the king.

Fa-la-la-la-la, he'll wear the signet ring.

"I need you to distract Haman," I whispered to Harold. "That way I can tell the rest of my family what's going on. He'll be nice to you if you give him a million compliments."

Harold pinched his hair spike. "Okay, if you think it will help." He strode up to Haman.

"Oh, great chief royal adviser," he said. "There is something of the utmost importance that you need to see in the kitchen. I urgently require your great knowledge and skills."

Haman smirked. "Well, I *am* the best chief royal advisor in the land. My knowledge and skills are unparalleled. Lead the way, small one."

Chapter Fifteen
Crazy Stories

As soon as Harold and Haman were in the kitchen, I marched up to Zadie. "We need to talk."

But my grandfather was busy dancing with the jesters. "Look, Saralee," he said, "they can juggle seven things at once. It's incredible."

"Seriously, Zadie, I need to tell—"

The jesters surrounded us, singing their silly songs. One did cartwheels, and the other two tossed spoons back and forth over our heads.

Dancing, prancing, and never-ending tricks
Ting-a-ling-a-ling, oh so merry
We'll have a little fun on this wondrous day
Come and celebrate, and don't you tarry.

Uncle Sam tried to juggle some spoons of his own, but they all clattered to the floor.

PLOP!

PLING!

PLAAAAAANG!

I'd had enough of this nonsense.

"STOP!!!!!!" I shouted at the top of my lungs.

The jesters froze in weird positions. One of them had a ridiculous look stuck on his face. Another flopped to the floor mid-cartwheel. And the third had a spoon balanced on the tip of his nose.

"It's Herman!" I cried. "He isn't a party coordinator. And he's not an actor. He's HAMAN!"

No one gasped. No one shouted. What was wrong with them? This was an emergency!

One of the jesters opened his mouth.

Fa-la-la-la-la—

"Stop singing," I snapped.

He closed his mouth. Tight.

Aunt Bean shook her head. "You're saying Herman is Haman from the Purim story? But how could Haman be *here* at Siegel House Restaurant?"

I let the words tumble out. "My hamantashen recipe has been summoning people and things from the Purim story. That's how we got the royal horse and these jesters. Herman is nice to adults, but as soon as he's just with kids, he's super-mean. He's been calling me and Josh tiny servants."

"Well, that certainly isn't nice," Aunt Bean said. "But that doesn't mean he's Haman."

Uncle Sam nodded. "Yeah, he made those thrones for Bubbie and Zadie, cooked us flatbread, and helped us with all the restaurant details. I don't think Haman would've done all that."

"Hey, where are my beanbag chairs for the

ancient doctor's office?" Josh cried. "There were three. Now they're gone."

But I didn't have time to worry about that. I had a real emergency on my hands.

"Zadie, you have to believe me. You can't hire Herman full-time at our restaurant. You just can't!"

Zadie knitted his eyebrows together. "Saralee, I'm concerned."

I let out the breath I'd been holding. Thank goodness Zadie believed me. He was always on my—

"Are you upset about Herman helping so much around the restaurant?" he asked. "I know he's done a lot of great stuff, like making the thrones and helping us with historical details. But that doesn't mean we don't appreciate all the stuff you're doing too."

A cold sensation grew in my stomach. It was like someone was crushing ice in there.

"Zadie, I'm telling you the truth! Herman is—"

The kitchen door swung open and Haman burst in. Harold rushed behind, a look of panic on his face.

"What's going on, my king?" said Haman. "I heard raised voices. Is everything all right?"

Inside, I felt like a potato exploding in the microwave.

"I know you're a bad guy," I shouted at Haman. "And I'm not going to stop until you're gone from our restaurant for good!"

Aunt Bean's eyes grew wide. Aunt Lotte's mouth dropped open. Uncle Sam rubbed his bald spot.

Haman gasped. "You accuse *me* of being

bad? I am no such thing. I am a loyal advisor to the great and mighty king."

"Saralee!" Zadie cried. "That was beyond disrespectful. You need to apologize."

Now I was angry at Zadie too. He believed Herman *over me*? I was his executive assistant. We'd been a perfect team for as long as I could remember. Didn't that count for anything?

"Never!" I cried.

Zadie put a hand on Haman's shoulder. "I am so sorry about this, Herman. I don't know what's gotten into her."

Harold stepped forward. "Look, she's telling the truth. We did an investi—"

Zadie held up his hand. "Harold, I think it's time for you to go home."

Harold looked at me helplessly. Then he picked up his backpack and headed for the door.

"She's telling the truth!" he shouted over his shoulder.

When he was gone, Herman cleared his throat.

"My king, it's clear that young Saralee is overworked and exhausted," he said smoothly. "Why don't you let *me* handle everything from now on? I am your chief royal advisor, after all."

A few tears spilled down my cheeks. Herman was so sneaky! He was twisting everything around.

"I'm fine," I yelled at Haman. "It's YOU that's the problem!"

"Oh, Saralee," Zadie sighed. "Maybe Herman's right. I've been putting too much pressure on you about that hamantashen recipe. Sometimes I forget—you're just a kid. I think you should take a break. We can figure out what's causing the bad taste next year."

This couldn't be happening! I didn't want to take a break! I loved being Zadie's executive assistant. Cooking and taste-testing and making jokes with Zadie were the best parts of my day.

"Saralee, did you hear me?" Zadie asked gently.

My nostrils flared. Just like in the Purim

story, Haman was manipulating the situation. And Zadie was falling for it!

Aunt Bean put a hand on my shoulder. "It's okay, Saralee. Everyone needs a little break sometimes."

"Yeah," Aunt Lotte chimed in. "I'd love a break."

"I . . . Zadie . . . ." I stuttered.

The jesters surrounded me and began harmonizing again.

Ting-a-ling-a-ling, it's time to take a break.
Ting-a-ling-a-ling, it's time to eat some cake.

But I didn't want to hear any of it. I pushed past the jesters and ran up to my room. With shaking fingers, I untied the strings of my executive-assistant apron and threw it onto the floor.

Only a few nights ago, Zadie had said that he could always count on me. And now he had just fired me from my job.

Chapter Sixteen
Back to His Own Time

The next day at school, I was in a terrible mood.

"Everything's a mess," I told Harold. "My family doesn't believe me about Haman, and now he's going to work at Siegel House full-time."

"I'm so sorry, Saralee," Harold said. "Want to come over today? We could brainstorm ways to get rid of him."

At lunch, I called home to tell my family

that I'd be at Harold's house after school. Aunt Bean picked up.

"That's fine," she said. "But do you want to talk to Zadie for a minute? He's right here. He wants to say hello to you."

I gripped the phone. I really *did* want to hear Zadie's voice. But . . . he'd taken Haman's side over mine. How could he? It felt like my heart had been crushed into a thousand tiny crumbs.

"No, I don't," I said. Then I made myself hang up.

After school, Harold and I went straight to Perfection on a Platter. The restaurant was decorated like a mixed-up fairy-tale. Glass slippers, "poison" apples, and vials of bright liquids gleamed in display cases. Even the seating hostess robot was dressed as a wicked witch!

The Horowitzes had programmed her to give an evil cackle.

MWAHAHA!

Harold and I sat in the dining room while his relatives rushed around with Purim preparations.

"We're excited for your royal party, Saralee," said one of Harold's uncles.

"Thanks," I said, even though my stomach was all knotted up just thinking about it. Between Haman and my gross Royal Hamantashen, Purim was shaping up to be a disaster.

Harold's mom, Mrs. Horowitz, burst out of the kitchen.

"Who didn't clean up all these dishes?" she yelled.

"Here we go again," Harold whispered to me. "She's dressing up as Cinderella's stepmother for Purim, and she's really getting into character."

Harold's uncle's face turned red. "You

know, I'm so tired of you bossing me around. It wouldn't hurt for you to—"

"This is your responsibility—"

"No, you said that *you* would do the dishes—"

"No I didn't."

"Yes you did."

They stomped into the kitchen, still bickering.

I sighed. "Looks like both of our families are having fights right now."

"Yeah," Harold said, "but I think it's okay to argue sometimes. I know my family can be intense, but that doesn't mean they don't love each other. And you and Zadie—haven't you ever had a fight before?"

Tears filled my eyes. "Not like this."

Harold put his arm around my shoulders. "Remember how we didn't get along when we first met? And now we're best friends forever. Just because you had a fight with Zadie doesn't mean everything is ruined between you guys."

I knew Harold was right. But my throat felt scratchy as I thought about what had happened yesterday.

"We need to figure out how to get rid of Haman," I said, my voice coming out all squeaky. "It's the only way to fix things with me and Zadie."

"Well, you're not the first girl who had to deal with Haman. What did Queen Esther do?"

I paused. "Esther invited the king and Haman to a banquet. Then she took a huge risk and told the king about Haman's terrible deeds. And she revealed that she was secretly Jewish too."

"Okay, since you've already tried telling your family about Haman, I guess you'll need to find a way to send him back to his own time," Harold said. "Could you do *that* at a banquet?"

I frowned. I'd brought Haman from the past through a smell. How could I . . .

Wait a minute!

Memories from the past few days flashed through my mind.

Could it be?

Every time I'd made my Royal Hamantashen recipe, something from the Purim story appeared at Siegel House. But something from Siegel House had ALSO disappeared. First the ice-cream maker, then the flowerpot, and then Josh's three beanbag chairs.

Maybe the smell swirls worked both ways. Maybe every time I summoned something from the Purim story, something from OUR time went back to ancient days. Which meant . . .

"Oh my goodness!" I cried. "I know exactly what to do!"

I told Harold about all the missing objects at Siegel House.

"So I *am* going to make a banquet, like Esther," I explained. "I'll make my Royal Hamantashen, the smell swirls will appear, and then I'll push Haman through the swirls to send him back to his own time."

Harold scratched his head. "But last time we made Royal Hamantashen, those smell swirls disappeared in like one second. I didn't even have the chance to see them."

I bit the nail of my pinkie. Harold was right. I had to make sure those smell swirls lasted a long time, so I could push Haman through.

Hmmm . . .

An idea popped into my head. But it was risky. Maybe just as risky as Esther's plan.

Until then, I'd only put the smells of the Purim story into *one recipe*—my Royal Hamantashen. But what would happen if I made an ENTIRE FEAST using the smells of the Purim story? Hopefully that would make the smell swirls super-large and long-lasting.

The only problem was . . . how many *more* things would I summon from the Purim story? And would anything else from Siegel House get sucked back in time?

This smell magic was so unpredictable. But I couldn't let Haman manipulate Zadie anymore. I had to be brave like Esther and stand up for what was right. Even if it was dangerous.

The kitchen door swung open.

"Harrrrrrold," called Mrs. Horowitz. "Your uncle seems to think that a fairy godmother will wash the dishes for him. Could you just do them? It's a mess in here, and I have so much to do. "

Harold sighed. "I guess I should help," he said.

"And I should go home," I said. "I can't wait a single second longer to send Haman back in time."

Chapter Seventeen
In Your Honor

I rushed home as fast as I could.

This would be the hardest part. I needed to *pretend* to be sorry to get my banquet plan to work.

When I found Zadie and "Herman" in the office, I did a double take. Haman was wearing a *triangular hat*.

"What do you mean by the word *computer*?" Haman asked. "Should we summon the royal mathematicians?"

Zadie sighed. "Herman, your acting has been wonderful. But seriously, this is crunch time. I need you to design and print out the menus. Playful Party Planners told me that you could do this."

Haman shook his head. "*Playful* Party Planners? I assure you that I take my role quite seriously, my king."

"Very funny, Herman." Zadie finally noticed me. "Saralee, I'm glad you're home. Are you okay? I wanted to talk to you about—"

"I'm fine," I interrupted. "Listen, I have something to say to you and Herman."

Haman leaned back in his chair. Now that he was off the hook about the computer, he was smirking again.

Just looking at him made my nostrils flare. But then I thought about how Queen Esther was so poised and brave when she faced Haman. I relaxed my nose.

"Look, Herman," I started. "I'm sorry for what I said yesterday. I know you've been working hard. You truly are an *amazing* chief royal advisor."

Haman puffed out his chest.

"Well that is certainly true," he said.

Zadie's face split into a smile. "I'm proud of you for saying that, Saralee."

"I really want to make it up to you, Herman," I continued. "So I'd like to invite you and Zadie to a banquet tonight in your honor. Something special, only for the king and his esteemed chief royal advisor. It's my way of saying thank you

103

for everything you've done for our family."

Haman stroked his beard. "A banquet *in my honor*," he said. "That is very fitting, especially after all the insults I endured yesterday."

Zadie nodded. "That is so thoughtful of you, Saralee. I think it's a great idea."

Zadie opened his arms for a big hug, and I let myself get wrapped up in his arms. It was nice to have my grandfather back. I could feel myself breathing easier now. Only, when I looked over Zadie's shoulder, Herman shot me a smirk.

My nostrils flared again.

Haman had no idea who he was messing with here. Using my super-nose, I would get rid of him for good.

Zadie let go, and I gave Haman an innocent smile. "Where did you get that interesting hat?" I asked.

"The king has a chest of royal accessories," he said. "It suits me perfectly. It reminds me of a hat I had at my previous palace. But it was misplaced in my travels. Now, for the banquet—"

Haman counted on his fingers. "I will have roasted artichokes, spicy noodle soup with vegetables, flatbread with oil and spices, mulled grape juice, and fig pudding."

"Ooh what a feast!" Zadie said.

"Of course, Herman," I said sweetly. "This will be the best banquet ever. Just you wait!"

Chapter Eighteen
Too Much to Handle

I got started on the banquet right away. I was going to make all of Haman's favorites—plus my Royal Hamantashen. My plan was to put the smells of the Purim story into every single dish.

Soon I got lost in the rhythm of cooking. I just let my super-nose lead the way. Before long, my nose was bursting with the incredible ancient scents!

Sweet!

Spicy!
Tangy!

The smells were so strong that my eyes began to water, and I had to wipe away the tears.

"Ohhhh, small one."

I whirled around. Haman had popped his head into the kitchen. "Make sure the mulled grape juice is *extra*-sweet," he said.

My hands curled into fists, but then I thought about Esther again. Even when Haman was trying to get rid of her entire people, Esther stayed calm so she could carry out her plan. She didn't yell and she didn't throw a fit.

Although she started off as a regular girl like me, she was a true queen—intelligent, brave, and poised.

If she could act that way, then so could I.

I took a deep breath and relaxed my hands. "Extra-sweet it is," I said.

It took me all afternoon and evening to prepare the banquet. I'd decided to make as many batches of Royal Hamantashen as I could. I needed the smells of the Purim story to be extra-strong.

But it was hard to keep my cool when Haman kept bothering me.

"What are these strange-looking pastries?" he asked, pointing to the hamantashen. "I didn't request these, tiny servant."

"I wanted to make you something extra-special, O great royal advisor," I said through gritted teeth. "I was inspired by the shape of your hat."

I had to use all three of the Siegel House ovens to bake all the food. When everything was almost ready, I set the kitchen table with a fancy tablecloth and dishes.

"Okay everyone," I called. "Your royal banquet awaits."

Zadie and Haman strode into the kitchen.

"Wow, smells great in here," said Zadie.

"Well of course, my king," said Haman. "We must eat the best food in all the land."

"Oh, this is nothing," I said sweetly. "It's about to smell a *lot* better."

Then I opened all three oven doors.

A rush of scents swirled into the kitchen. The smells of the Purim story were *much* stronger this time.

"This is incredible," gushed Zadie. "The smells are so powerful! One sniff and I'm transported to the real palace."

Haman frowned. "My king, what do you mean by the *real* palace?"

I glanced at the oven. Those silver swirls were

back, but this time they were much, MUCH bigger. They slithered out of the oven like giant silver snakes. My plan had worked!

Zadie pressed his hand to his chest. "Goodness gracious, what are those things?"

Haman gasped and backed up against the wall. "What is this? All . . . all that stuff . . . It's so familiar . . . ."

The images inside the swirls were much clearer than before: a banquet hall filled with royal guests, a library stuffed with ancient books, the palace courtyard, and hallways lined with portraits.

This was my chance to get rid of Haman for good. But before I could push him into the swirls—

CRASH!

An ancient warrior statue had crushed one of the chairs at the kitchen island.

"Ah!" I jumped back, and Zadie shielded my head with his arms. Haman cowered behind the garbage can.

"Saralee, what's going on?" Zadie cried.

The smells of the Purim story were truly staggering. This was way too much for my super-nose to handle! I gripped the side of the countertop, trying to breathe normally. "It's—"

A tapestry flapped through the air. Jugs of grape juice shattered on the floor. Ancient coins rained down on us, and a parrot swooped overhead.

"Aaaaah!" we screamed.

"Squawk!" cried the parrot.

A harp hurtled toward me. I rolled out of

the way, and it slammed into the wall.

"Help!" cried Haman. He used the broom to bat a goblet away, and it flew toward Zadie's head.

"Zadie, watch out!" I screamed.

Zadie ducked just in time. "Careful with that broom, Herman!" he cried.

The silver swirls twisted inward, and wind whipped through the kitchen. The swirls were turning into a *smell vortex*!

Chapter Nineteen
Smell Vortex

Everything was chaos. I watched in horror as the dishes on the table, the napkin holder, and the salt and pepper shakers rattled in their spots. Then, in an instant, they flew into the smell swirls.

This whole situation was getting out of control!

The wind lashed at my face. A basket of fruit sailed through the air, straight into the swirls. In exchange, the swirls spit out a few scrolls.

"Make it stop, Saralee!" Zadie cried.

The toaster flew off the counter. Pots and pans dashed through the air. The cabinet doors slammed open and closed. Drawers whizzed out of the cupboards.

The vortex kept spitting out more things from the Purim story: serving platters, fresh flowers, chopped wood, dresses.

"Save meeeeee. Help!!!" sobbed Haman. He grasped the kitchen island and ended up between me and Zadie.

The door burst open, and the rest of my family and the jesters streamed into the kitchen.

"Oh my goodness! What's going on?" Aunt Bean cried.

"Get back," Zadie shouted. "It could pull you in!"

One of the jesters broke out in song:

Whirling, whirling, there's a storm inside
Ting-a-ling-a-ling, oh so scary

The jesters tried to dance in the wind, but the smell vortex was sucking them in.

Swirling, twirling, waltzing in the—

The swirls surrounded the jesters and they disappeared.

Holy moly, this wind was strong!

There was no time to lose. I needed to make sure Haman went through the smell vortex, but I didn't want to get sucked in myself! My arms shook as I gripped the island. This was the moment of truth: I needed to be brave like Esther and get rid of Haman for good.

Using all of my strength and balance, I took one hand off the kitchen island.

"Stop, Saralee," called Zadie. "What are you doing?"

"Don't let go," Aunt Bean shrieked.

"It's not safe," Uncle Sam hollered.

But I had to do this. Otherwise, we'd never get rid of Haman.

"I'm not a tiny servant," I yelled at Haman. "I'm sending you away. Don't you EVER come back to Siegel House."

Haman sneered. "You insolent little—"

Before he could finish, I pushed him as hard as I could toward the swirls.

Haman's hands slipped off the island, and he wobbled backward. "You terrible tiny servant, I will get my revenge!" He grabbed Zadie's arm.

"Let go of him," I snarled.

"Easy, Herman!" said Zadie.

The swirls were dangerously close, and the images inside were crystal clear. There was the king and his royal court. And one of the men in the court was clearly "Herman."

Zadie saw it too. His eyes grew wide.

"You *really are* Haman," he gasped. "Oh no—"

The silver swirls pulled Herman AND Zadie into the vortex. Zadie's salt-and-pepper hair was blowing every which way. "Zadie!!!" I screamed. "No!"

"Saraleeeeeeee!" Zadie cried.

The vortex let out a terrible roar, and Haman and Zadie disappeared.

Chapter Twenty
Only You

The smell vortex still raged around me. I squeezed my eyes shut, willing this all to be a dream.

"Saralee, watch out!" boomed Uncle Sam.

My eyes flew open. The smell swirls were only inches from my face. If I didn't find a way to stop the smell vortex, I would get pulled in too.

"Open the window!" I yelled. "We need to let out the smells!"

Uncle Sam lunged at the window and shoved it open.

A cool breeze filtered into the room, and the vortex dissolved into gentle swirls. The cabinet doors stopped opening and closing. The drawers lay still. The parrot stopped zooming around the kitchen and perched on the harp.

"Squawk!"

I sank to the floor, which was littered with scrolls, musical instruments, chopped wood, and flowers.

This couldn't be happening! Sure, Haman was gone. But my sweet, sweet Zadie was gone, too. My family surrounded me.

"Are you okay?" Aunt Bean asked.

"What just happened?" asked Aunt Lotte.

I opened my mouth, but no words came out.

Josh put a dish towel around my shoulders. "It's okay, Saralee. Do you want a bandage?"

Bubbie patted my hair.

Slowly, I was able to answer my family's questions.

"So let me get this straight," said Uncle Sam. "Herman really was Haman. And now Zadie is . . . *in the Purim story?*"

"Yeah," I said, quietly. "That's where the jesters and the horse came from too."

"So everything you said before was true," gasped Aunt Bean.

I surveyed the kitchen and winced at the damage. Junk was strewn everywhere, the cabinets were all wonky, and there were big dents in the floor. But the feast I'd made for Zadie and Herman was untouched. All seven batches of hamantashen were in perfect condition.

I guess it made sense. During a hurricane, the center of the storm is calm. And the food had been the center of the smell vortex.

"But you can get Zadie back out of the story, right?" asked Uncle Sam.

"I don't know," I said. I felt numb all over, as if

120

someone had covered my body in ice packs.

"But you'll try?" asked Aunt Lotte. "Because you're the only one with a super-nose. Only you can get Zadie back out of the Purim story."

A terrible thought flashed through my mind. What if I couldn't figure it out? What if Zadie was gone forever?

Chapter Twenty-One
The Gift Basket

The next day, there was no school so the community could get ready for Purim. As soon as I opened my eyes, it all came flooding back.

Zadie was gone. And it was all my fault.

Downstairs, Aunt Bean had scrubbed the kitchen clean. There was still a big dent in the floor, but she'd fixed all the cupboards and cabinets as best as she could. The parrot was perched on the giant harp again, and Aunt Lotte was feeding it almonds.

Breakfast wasn't the same without Zadie. Uncle Sam made eggs, but they were burnt and smelled like stinky feet. Bubbie made coffee, but Zadie wasn't there to drink it.

No one was talking, not even when we all gathered at the kitchen table.

"We're canceling the Purim party, right?" I finally asked.

Aunt Bean and Uncle Sam glanced at each other.

"I think that's what's best," Uncle Sam said. "We can let the customers know when we're done eating."

"Yeah, we can't have a Purim without Zadie," Josh agreed.

I stared at my burnt, rubbery eggs. I wasn't hungry.

KNOCK, KNOCK.

"I'll get it," I sighed.

I opened the door to find Harold on the front steps, holding a basket of food and drinks.

"Hey," he said. "Did your plan work? Is Herman gone?"

"Yeah, Herman's gone," I mumbled. "But so is Zadie."

Harold's mouth dropped open. "WHAT?"

In a rush, I told him everything.

Harold pinched his hair spike. "There has to be a way to get him back, right? Can I help?"

My voice came out all wobbly. "I don't know, Harold. If I make the Royal Hamantashen again, something *else* from the Purim story could come out. And who knows what would go back in its place?"

"I'm so sorry," Harold said. "I know how much Zadie means to you. He's such a cool grandpa."

I nodded, trying not to cry.

Harold handed me

the basket. "I know this won't help, but I made you mishlo'ach manot."

Mishlo'ach manot are gift baskets people give to their friends and family on Purim. "Harold, I'm sorry. I don't have one for you," I said. "Things have just been so crazy, I forgot."

"That's okay," said Harold. "And if there's something I can do to help with all this, you'll call me, right?"

A few tears streamed down my cheeks. I wiped them away before Harold could see. "Th-thanks, I will."

He walked back down the steps, and I closed the door. I sat at one of the tables in the restaurant dining room to open the mishlo'ach manot.

I had to smile when I saw what was inside. Harold's an amazing pastry artist. He'd made a dozen sugar cookies with different designs: poison apples, crowns, and magic wands.

Tucked inside the basket was a small white envelope. I opened it and found a card decorated with Little Red Riding Hood and the Big Bad Wolf.

Happy Purim, Saralee, Harold had written. *Good thing you didn't sniff out the smells in* **this** *story. It would've been terrifying if you'd brought the wolf to life! So glad you're my friend. Love, Harold.*

I put down the card and sniffed the poison apple cookies. They were covered with cinnamon sugar. Harold's creations were so—

Wait a minute!

I picked up the card and read it again.

Good thing you didn't sniff out the smells in **this** *story.*

My heart raced. Could that be the answer? Could stories be the key?

Maybe there *was* a way for me to bring Zadie home!

Chapter Twenty-Two
The Best Story

I ran back to the kitchen.

"I think I know how to bring Zadie back," I blurted.

"Are you serious?" asked Uncle Sam.

Aunt Bean popped out of her chair. "How?"

"The first time I made my Royal Hamantashen, I tried capturing *the story* of Purim through smell," I explained. "If I can sniff out the smells of the Purim story, what's stopping me from capturing the smells of a different story? The story of me and Zadie!"

"That's a good idea," said Josh.

"What're you gonna make?" asked Aunt Lotte. "Because I could use a second breakfast after those stinky eggs."

"Another batch of hamantashen," I said. "Can you guys help me find the ingredients for a new hamantashen filling? I'll shout them out to you."

Bubbie nodded. "Of course, Pookie Wookie. Of course."

I put on my executive assistant apron and tied a dishtowel around my eyes and ears. Everything grew dark and quiet.

Hmmmmm, the story of me and Zadie . . .

My nose was bombarded with the smells of Haman's royal banquet from yesterday. But I pushed those smells away. Gradually, new images came into focus.

There I was, as a toddler, sitting in Zadie's lap as he read to me from a stack of papers.

"These are the top secret family recipes," he said,

ruffling toddler-Saralee's hair. "Ooh, let's start with this one: my mother's lemon sponge cake."

Toddler-Saralee clapped her hands and giggled. Even back then, Zadie and I had a special connection.

Then the scene changed, and the whole family was at the dinner table. Zadie handed four-year-old-Saralee a bowl of golden carrot soup, and she took a big sniff.

"I know everything in here," said four-year-old-Saralee.

Zadie narrowed his eyes. "What do you mean?"

Four-year-old-Saralee smiled and said, "two cups of leeks, two-and-a-half pounds of carrots, three pink apples, four cups of vegetable stock, two cups of apple cider, one teaspoon of turmeric, a pinch of cinnamon, a knob of ginger, a splash of coconut milk, a squeeze of honey, and a little black pepper sprinkled on top."

Zadie's eyes grew wide. "You smelled all that?"

The scents of Zadie's soup enveloped me like a warm hug. Zadie's face lit up with pride. This was the day he learned about my super-nose!

The smells carried me to the next scene. Now I was eight years old, when I became Zadie's executive assistant. We cooked and laughed and taste-tested together. The smells were soft and sweet and comforting.

"What's your favorite hamantashen flavor, Zadie?" eight-year-old Saralee asked.

Zadie grinned. "Chocolate, of course. What's yours?"

Eight-year-old

Saralee paused. "Well . . . I love so many. Apricot, peanut butter, caramel. But I think my favorite is raspberry."

Zadie put his arm around eight-year-old Saralee. "You know, raspberries and chocolate go perfectly together."

"Then let's make a filling with both!"

I wanted to stay here forever, surrounded by the incredible scents. But the images began to fade, and I opened my eyes.

"Lemon zest," I called. "A smidgen of grated carrot, chocolate, raspberry jam, and . . . "

My family bustled around the kitchen, grabbing the right ingredients.

"Anything else?" asked Aunt Lotte. "Or is that it?"

I shook my head. "I'm not sure."

My super-nose knew the recipe needed something else, but I wasn't sure what yet.

Uncle Sam handed me a mixing bowl, and Josh helped me combine the ingredients. The hamantashen filling smelled wonderful, but it still wasn't quite right.

I squeezed my eyes shut, trying to think.

Maybe our story had a second part?

All my life, Zadie had taken such good care of me. He'd been my whole world. I loved him so much. And he loved me too.

For so long, I believed that we'd always get along perfectly. But then Haman showed up and we had a real fight. I never thought that would happen, not in a million bazillion years.

And now, I couldn't help but wonder if things were different between us. Did we love each other the same way as before?

A warm and fuzzy feeling pushed its way into my heart. It grew stronger and stronger until I was absolutely bursting with it.

The answer was clear.

Yes, I still loved Zadie. And he still loved me. And yes, things were different now, but not in a bad way. Our love was stronger *after* our fight because I knew we could overcome any challenge.

Something inside me clicked. Without thinking about it, I poured everything I felt for Zadie into the hamantashen recipe. All the love in my heart streamed into my mixing bowl.

I opened my eyes. My family was staring at me. "You okay, Saralee?" asked Josh.

I grinned at him. "Better than okay."

The terrible emptiness inside me was gone. Instead, I felt as if Zadie was in the kitchen beside me, holding my hand.

Chapter Twenty-Three
Group Hug

Twenty minutes later, the hamantashen were golden brown.

I opened the oven door, and a surge of flavors swooshed into the air.

Bubbie took a huge sniff. "My stars, so many feelings in that smell."

Aunt Lotte nodded. "It's so comforting."

"And happy!" Josh chimed in.

When I took out the tray, the silver swirls appeared again. There was toddler-Saralee, four-year-old-Saralee, and executive-assistant-Saralee—and each version of me was with Zadie.

"Woah, what are those images?" asked Uncle Sam. "Is that you and Zadie?"

I nodded. "It's our story."

Just before the images faded into nothingness, an image of Haman flashed in the swirls as well. I guess he was part of our story now. Haman had taught me that sometimes Zadie and I wouldn't get along. And that was okay.

Aunt Bean handed out the hamantashen. One for each of us.

"On the count of three," she said. "One . . . two . . . three!"

I took a bite, and it tasted incredible. One moment it was lemon, the next raspberry-chocolate, the next pink apple.

"Scrumptious." Uncle Sam grabbed a second cookie.

Aunt Bean wiped crumbs off the counter before taking a second bite. "Divine," she said.

"So yummy," cried Josh.

"By golly, Pookie Wookie," said Bubbie. "What a treat!"

Even Aunt Lotte was impressed. "Not bad, Saralee," she said. Then she gave a tiny piece to the parrot on her shoulder.

CRASH!

We all looked at each other. "Could it be?" said Aunt Bean.

Fast as we could, we ran to the dining room, where we found—

"Zadie!" I cried.

My grandfather stood in the center of the dining room, wearing a fancy robe. His salt-and-pepper hair was messy from the smell swirls, but otherwise he looked unchanged.

"Home sweet home," Zadie sighed.

136

I threw myself into his arms. "You're back! You're finally back!"

My family gathered around us and piled in for a group bear hug.

"Oh, thank goodness," sighed Aunt Bean.

"We missed you," said Josh.

"I'm getting squished," Zadie laughed.

But everyone just hugged him even tighter.

When we finally let go, Zadie took a sniff. "Golly, it smells incredible in here. It reminds me of all these memories."

"I made a new hamantashen recipe to bring you back," I said. "I know it doesn't smell like the Purim story. But I think this one is so much—"

"Saralee," he said, his voice cracking. "It's perfect. And you were right about everything. I'm so sorry—"

"Were you in the Purim story? What did you see?" Aunt Lotte blurted.

"Did you meet the royal doctor?" asked Josh. "Did you see anyone with measles or small pockets?"

137

"And what about Herman?" asked Aunt Bean.

"Goodness gracious," said Zadie. "Slow down!"

Uncle Sam helped Zadie to his royal throne. Bubbie sat next to him and took his hand.

"Let me start from the beginning," Zadie said. "As soon as we got to the Purim story, I knew I'd been a fool. Saralee was telling the truth all along—Herman *really was* Haman. So I helped Queen Esther catch him. She put Haman in the dungeon and treated me like a guest of honor."

"What happened next?" I asked.

"Esther invited me to a banquet, and I told her all about you guys. Especially my courageous granddaughter. Oh goodness, Saralee, you should have smelled the feast she made!"

Zadie looked at his watch. "Golly, is that the time? We have to get ready for tonight's party!"

"But the party's canceled," I said.

"We couldn't possibly have a party without you," said Aunt Bean.

Zadie grinned. "Well, I'm back now, aren't I? Did you already call the customers?"

"Not yet," said Aunt Lotte.

Zadie stood up and stretched. "Then I'm officially un-canceling the Purim party. Let's get a move on, folks. We have a lot to do!"

We all sprang into action.

Aunt Bean set the tables with the royal dishes from the smell vortex. Uncle Sam set up the carnival games on the front lawn. Aunt Lotte, parrot still on her shoulder, groomed the horse. Bubbie decorated the ancient warrior statue with dried noodles. And Josh added the scrolls and coins to his royal physician office.

"Now the guests can pretend to pay me!" he said.

In the kitchen, Zadie and I made chicken pomegranate stew, cucumber and mint salad, and a huge batch of crispy rice. Of course, there was plenty of food from yesterday's banquet as well.

We cooked, and cooked, and cooked until there was only one thing left to discuss.

"So what about the hamantashen?" I asked.

There were two kinds on the counter: one that told the story of Purim and one that told the story of Zadie and me.

"I wonder . . . " Zadie picked up one of my Royal Hamantashen.

"Stop!" I cried. "I was going to throw them out. They're awful!"

But Zadie took a big bite. He chewed thoughtfully.

"It tastes wonderful, Saralee," he said. "Here—you try one."

I nibbled on one of the Royal Hamantashen. An incredible taste filled my mouth—bold and bright, changing from sweet, to spicy, to tangy, and back again.

I chewed and chewed and chewed, but the terrible taste never came. How could this be?

"Wait a minute," I cried. "It must have been *Haman* who made my hamantashen taste so bad.

When he showed up, everything became rotten and terrible—just like in the Purim story."

Zadie nodded. "The more powerful he got here, the worse your hamantashen tasted. Now that he's gone, they're just plain delicious."

It all made perfect sense.

"Let's serve both," said Zadie. "Your Royal Hamantashen and your new hamantashen. They tell the stories of *two* strong ladies who stood up to Haman."

I grinned. "Perfect."

Chapter Twenty-Four

Together Forever

"**H**ere they come," cried Aunt Bean, pointing out the window. It was late afternoon, and we all wore our royal outfits. A crowd was gathering outside Siegel House Restaurant. Harold and his whole family were at the front of the line— dressed in their villainous fairy-tale costumes, of course.

Everyone scrambled to their stations. Josh went to his physician's office. Uncle Sam stood by the carnival games. Aunt Bean elegantly folded the last napkin. Aunt Lotte held the royal horse's reins as the horse nuzzled her ear. And I finished arranging the platters of hamantashen.

Zadie opened the front door.

"Good evening, my esteemed guests," he said, with a sweep of his arm. "Welcome to Siegel Palace."

Rachel Rubin dashed over to the horse and stroked his long mane. Jacob Brodsky was first in line for bowling on the front lawn. Bubbie played the harp (which surprised everyone), and the guests oohed and aahed over the royal decorations.

Mrs. Baum sat on a royal throne. The parrot perched on the back of her chair. "How did you get a real parrot?" she asked.

"Squawk!" went the parrot.

Mr. Alkana examined an ancient scroll. "This looks very authentic. Almost as if it's from the Purim story itself!"

Zadie and I handed out the hamantashen as an appetizer. I walked over to Harold, who was busy playing royal physician with Josh.

"Hello, kind sir," I said. "Would you like some hamantashen?"

"Sure!" he said. "And I see Zadie is back, thank goodness. I knew you could do it!"

"It's actually because of something you said. Well, actually—something you wrote," I explained.

Harold blinked a few times. "Really?"

"I must check for measles," Josh blurted, pulling on Harold's arm.

"I'll tell you later," I whispered.

"Just one second, Josh," Harold laughed. "I want to try the hamantashen." He took a royal-flavored one and looked at it suspiciously. "Are these . . . you know, safe?"

"They are now," I promised. "It turned out that Haman was making them taste so awful. Now that he's gone, they're delicious!"

Harold took a bite. "Wow," he said. "Unbelievable. It makes me feel like I'm really inside the story."

Then he took a second cookie—one that told

the story of me and Zadie. He nibbled the corner. "You know, I like your Royal Hamantashen," he said. "But I think this one is better. It makes me feel all warm and fuzzy inside. I taste raspberries and chocolate and . . . something else. What did you put in it again?"

I glanced at Zadie, who was surrounded by guests. "Oh, dearest people, have some more hamantashen," he boomed.

I turned back to Harold. "Well, each of my hamantashen tells a story," I explained. "And this one tells the story of me and Zadie."

"Cool," said Harold. "Your food is always so—"

"Attention! Attention!" Uncle Sam interrupted. "It's time to read the Purim story. Please take your seats."

Everyone rushed to the tables as Uncle Sam took out a large scroll with fancy Hebrew letters. Harold motioned for me to sit next to him, but Zadie grabbed my hand.

"Now hold on a minute," he whispered in my ear.

145

"Before we hear the story, I think we should chat."

As Zadie led me to the kitchen, my heart beat like a drum. We'd been so busy with Purim preparations, we hadn't gotten a chance to *really* talk earlier. I had no idea what Zadie was about to say.

"Saralee, I'm so sorry I didn't believe you about Haman," Zadie said softly. "I didn't see him for who he was. He promised to help me get all the details right, and I got so lost in that, even when you tried to warn me."

I swallowed. It felt so good to hear Zadie say that. "Apology accepted. And I'm sorry that I accidentally sent you into the Purim story. I didn't mean to put you in danger, Zadie . . . can you forgive me?"

Zadie wrapped his arm around me. "Of course. I know you were just trying to do the right thing. By the way, I think the best part of this whole experience was seeing ancient people trying to make sense of an ice-cream machine. All of our missing stuff ended up in the Purim story! Crazy, right?"

I giggled.

"Speaking of which, I have a few things to give you," Zadie said.

Eyes sparkling, he reached into the pocket of his robe and withdrew something wrapped in cloth. "This is from Esther. When I told her about you, she insisted on giving you a gift. To reward you for your bravery, of course."

Slowly, I unwrapped the present. It was a tiara! "Wow . . . Zadie, thank you. I can't believe it's actually from Queen Esther!"

I put it on. Even though it was covered in jewels, it felt light and airy on my head.

But Zadie wasn't done yet. He reached back into his pocket. "And *this* is from me. When I saw it at the royal feast, I knew I had to bring it home for you."

I took a tiny sniff with my super-nose.

"Ohhh, I know what that is," I said.

Zadie held out a small peapod.

"Open it," he said.

I gently peeled it open. Two peas sat side by side.

"One of them is me and the other one is you," he said.

I grinned at Zadie, and he grinned back. He smelled like he always did: peppermint with a hint of corned beef on rye.

"Together forever?" he asked.

I squeezed Zadie's hand, and he squeezed back.

"Of course," I said. "Together forever—two peas in a pod."

The End

Saralee and Zadie's Hamantashen Recipe

Makes approximately 4 dozen hamantashen

Before making these delicious hamantashen, ask an adult for permission.
Always have an adult help when you need to use the oven.

Ingredients

Dough
1 cup sugar
1 cup butter (softened)
3 eggs
¼ teaspoon salt
⅓ cup orange juice
2 teaspoons vanilla
4 cups flour
1 tablespoon baking powder

Filling
½ cup raspberry jam/preserves
Semisweet chocolate chips

Directions

1. Using an electric mixer, cream together sugar and butter. Add eggs and mix.

2. Add the rest of the dough ingredients in the order listed and mix.

3. Cover and refrigerate for a minimum of 3 hours.

4. To assemble, roll out dough on a floured board to ¼-inch thick. The dough will be sticky, so make sure to flour the board well!

5. Cut the dough into rounds using a cookie cutter or upside-down glass.

6. Put ½ teaspoon raspberry jam on each cookie round. Place 4-5 chocolate chips on top.

7. Fold over and pinch together to form a triangle.

8. Placed on a greased cookie sheet.

9. Bake at 350°F for 17 minutes or until browned.